Little, Brown and Company
Hachette Book Group
1290 Avenue of the Americas, New York, NY 10104
Visit us at LBYR.com
mylittlepony.com

First Edition: September 2019

LB kids is an imprint of Little, Brown and Company.
The LB kids name and logo are trademarks of Hachette Book Group, Inc.

The publisher is not responsible for websites (or their content) that are not owned by the publisher.

Library of Congress Control Number 2018942739

ISBNs: 978-0-316-51857-4 (pbk.), 978-0-316-51862-8 (ebook), 978-0-316-51866-6 (ebook), 978-0-316-51859-8 (ebook)

Printed in China

APS

10 9 8 7 6 5 4 3 2

Licensed By:

Princess Celestia's Starring Role

Based on the episode "Horse Play"
by **Kaita Mpambara**
Adapted by **Louise Alexander**

LITTLE, BROWN & COMPANY
LB kids

A very special day was coming in Equestria—the 1,111th year anniversary of when Princess Celestia first raised the sun over her kingdom.

Princess Twilight Sparkle and Spike proposed putting on a play to celebrate!

Princess Celestia was so excited. "A play is a fantastic idea! When I was a filly, I was too busy to be part of any plays. I always wanted to experience the special friendships formed in the theater."

Twilight Sparkle had an idea.
"Princess Celestia, would you do
us the honor of starring in our play?"
Both Celestia and Spike were shocked.

"Are you sure?" Celestia asked. "It's a dream of mine to be onstage, but I don't have any acting experience!"

Twilight Sparkle ignored her doubts. "You'll be playing yourself, so you have plenty of experience! Plus, all the ponies will help you. Please—it would mean so much to us!"

Celestia jumped for joy. "I would be delighted to join your theater troupe!"

At the theater, Twilight shared the news with the cast and crew. Not only had Princess Celestia approved the play...she'd be the star of the show!

Rainbow Dash got so excited that she immediately jetted off. "This play is going to be amazing! I'm going to tell everypony I know!"

The other ponies were a little more worried about having the princess around.

"We have to take everything to the next level. None of our old ideas will do!" Rarity said.

"What if we sweat or need to blow our noses around her?" asked Starlight Glimmer.

"Celestia just wants to experience the bonding that comes with putting on a play," Twilight said calmly. "You should be yourselves!"

Applejack nodded. "Y'all are fretting over nothing. What could go wrong?"

When rehearsals started, everything was amazing!
Everything...except the star of the show!

First Celestia said her lines
too quietly. Then too loudly.
No matter what directions
Twilight offered, the princess
just couldn't get it right.

Dance practice didn't go much better.

Celestia tossed a prop through the air, and it accidentally hit a switch that sent half the cast *and* the centerpiece of the set plummeting though a trapdoor.

The beautiful, glittering sun was shattered!

Backstage, Twilight paced. "I can't tell Celestia she's terrible, but if I don't say anything our play will be a laughingstock!"

"You've gotta tell the truth, Twilight. It's a huge part of friendship," advised Applejack.

"So is making somepony's dreams come true." Twilight Sparkle had a plan. She knew she could fix this.

Twilight organized a private workshop for Celestia with Equestria's famed acting teachers, the Method Mares.

Celestia was so grateful. "This is the special stagepony bond of trust and honesty I always wanted, Twilight!"
Twilight hoped this would help.

But that hope vanished when the workshop started. Raspberry Beret and Onstage tried every acting exercise they could think of. They started with improvisation.

Then visualization. Raspberry Beret pretended she was skiing.

They even tried charades! Nothing they did could hide the fact that acting was simply not one of Celestia's talents.

In the meantime, the other ponies worked behind the scenes to find a replacement sun.
They tried blowing up a balloon.

They tried roasting a giant marshmallow.

They even tried using a ball of fireworks!
But each try only damaged the set even more!

Twilight Sparkle was so frustrated. She tried to keep it in, but all her emotions came out in one giant eruption right before the play was supposed to start.

"*ARRGGGG!* Everything is going wrong, from the stage to the props to the WORST. LEAD. ACTRESS. IN. *EQUESTRIAAAAA!*"

"Worst lead actress? I can't believe you didn't tell me you thought my acting was awful!" Twilight turned around. Oh no! Celestia had heard *everything*. "I thought I taught you about the importance of friendship, trust, and honesty."

Before Twilight could respond, Celestia flew away.

Twilight Sparkle followed, leaving the crew to stall the start of the show.

"Princess Celestia," she called, catching up to her, "you've always guided me, and I've looked up to you since I was a filly! I just wanted to give something back to you. I'm so sorry."

"Twilight, while you had good intentions, and while I appreciate you supporting me," Celestia said, "you know the truth is always better than a well-meant lie."

"I know I should have told you the truth in the first place, but I didn't want to disappoint you," Twilight replied.

"Isn't there a saying in the theater...the show must go on? If we don't hurry back, you'll disappoint your audience!" Celestia smiled. Twilight smiled back.

Together, the Alicorns returned to the theater and strode backstage. Celestia was ready to take charge.

"Rarity, Applejack, Pinkie Pie, Twilight!" Celestia said. "Calm the audience and let them know we're about to get started!"

The princess continued, "Starlight, do you have a copy of the script?

"Rainbow Dash, bring us some clouds for our new backdrop!

"Spike, you're our narrator!"

It turned out that being a princess prepared Celestia for being a great director!

"Fluttershy," Celestia continued, "you'll be our new lead!"

Fluttershy's eyes grew wide, and she shook her head wildly. "Me...playing you...while you watch me...playing you?! Oh no, I couldn't possibly do that! I have too much stage fright!"

"Visualize with me." Celestia used the tools she learned in her acting class. "You're a princess. Commanding. Confident. *Feel* the rising sun's warmth. Equestria needs you!"

Thanks to Rainbow Dash spreading the word across Equestria, the curtain opened to a packed audience.

Spike started, "Once upon a time—"

But the audience interrupted him! They laughed and made fun of the makeshift set and costumes.

Spike started sweating nervously. "Improvise!" Celestia whispered.

With the princess's instruction, Spike began adding his own humorous touch to the script. Soon enough the audience was laughing again…in a good way!

Fluttershy made a gorgeous entrance. Her mane shimmered with color and glitter as she proclaimed, "It's time for a new day in Equestria!"

Behind the scenes, Twilight was still panicking. The cast hadn't been able to replace the sun for the final scene!

Celestia whispered from the side of the stage. "Charades, Fluttershy! Use a regal gesture to show them the sun!"

Fluttershy raised her hoof majestically, just as Celestia said.

Suddenly, the *real* sun magically rose up in the sky, casting a brilliant glow over the production!

The audience roared with applause. The cast was showered in flowers tossed from the adoring crowd. Bravo, ponies! The play was a success!

"Thank you for saving our play, Princess Celestia,"
said Twilight Sparkle gratefully.

"I feel bad that you weren't in it, though," Fluttershy added.

The princess smiled. "I never felt I had to be onstage to be part of the show. Even working behind the scenes was a dream come true.

"And none of you need to call me *Princess* anymore," Celestia continued. "I had so much fun, I've decided to give up my crown and devote all my time to theater!"
The ponies gasped.

"Gotcha!" Princess Celestia winked. "Maybe I'm not such a bad actress after all."

As the ponies laughed, Celestia smiled. All she really wanted was to share the experience of creativity and happiness with her friends. In that sense, the play went exactly as planned.